D0033968

# WELCOME TO
# PASSPORT TO READING
### A beginning reader's ticket to a brand-new world!

Every book in this program is designed to build read-along and read-alone skills, level by level, through engaging and enriching stories. As the reader turns each page, he or she will become more confident with new vocabulary, sight words, and comprehension.

These PASSPORT TO READING levels will help you choose the perfect book for every reader.

**READING TOGETHER**
Read short words in simple sentence structures together to begin a reader's journey.

**READING OUT LOUD**
Encourage developing readers to sound out words in more complex stories with simple vocabulary.

**READING INDEPENDENTLY**
Newly independent readers gain confidence reading more complex sentences with higher word counts.

**READY TO READ MORE**
Readers prepare for chapter books with fewer illustrations and longer paragraphs.

This book features sight words from the educator-supported Dolch Sight Word List. Readers will become more familiar with these commonly used vocabulary words, increasing reading speed and fluency.

For more information, please visit www.passporttoreadingbooks.com, where each reader can add stamps to a personalized passport while traveling through story after story!

*Enjoy the journey!*

HASBRO and its logo, TRANSFORMERS and all related characters are trademarks of Hasbro and are used with permission. © 2012 Hasbro. All Rights Reserved.

In accordance with the U.S. Copyright Act of 1976, the scanning, uploading, and electronic sharing of any part of this book without the permission of the publisher is unlawful piracy and theft of the author's intellectual property. If you would like to use material from the book (other than for review purposes), prior written permission must be obtained by contacting the publisher at permissions@hbgusa.com. Thank you for your support of the author's rights.

Little, Brown and Company

Hachette Book Group
237 Park Avenue, New York, NY 10017
Visit our website at www.lb-kids.com

Little, Brown and Company is a division of Hachette Book Group, Inc.
The Little, Brown name and logo are trademarks of Hachette Book Group, Inc.

The publisher is not responsible for websites (or their content)
that are not owned by the publisher.

First Edition: September 2012

ISBN 978-0-316-18864-7

10 9 8 7 6 5 4 3 2 1

IM

Printed in China

LICENSED BY:

# TRANSFORMERS PRIME

## DECEPTICON IN DISGUISE

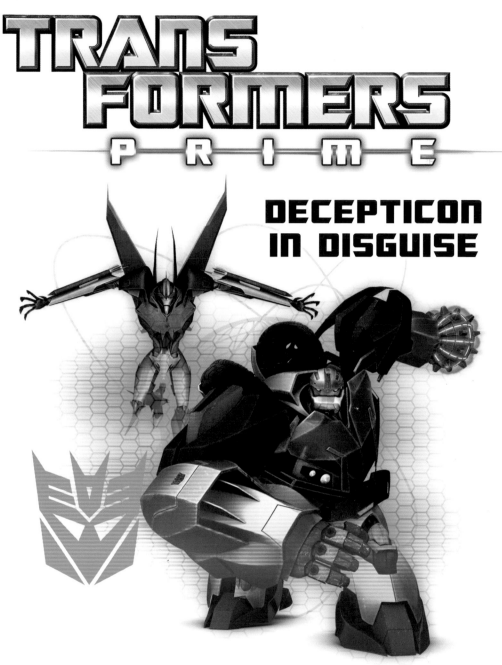

*Adapted by* Katharine Turner

*Based on the episode "Con Job"*
*written by* Steven Melching

**LITTLE, BROWN AND COMPANY**
New York  Boston

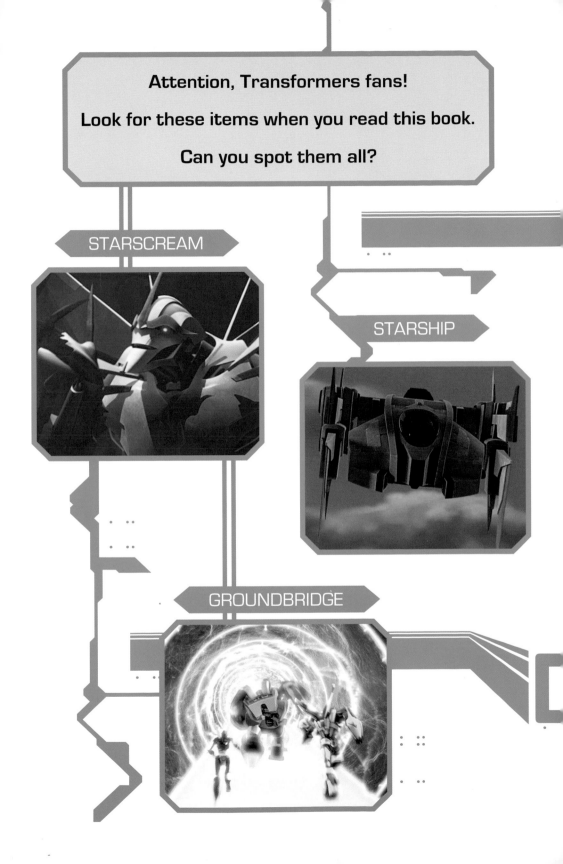

Attention, Transformers fans!

Look for these items when you read this book.

Can you spot them all?

STARSCREAM

STARSHIP

GROUNDBRIDGE

The Autobots are in their secret base
when they receive a message from a faraway starship.
"It appears to be an Autobot beacon," says Ratchet.
"Open up a line to talk to them," orders Optimus Prime.
"Unknown vessel, please identify yourself."

"What a welcome!" says the traveler.

Bulkhead recognizes the voice right away.

It is his best friend, Wheeljack!

"How soon can you get here, buddy?" asks Bulkhead.

"Tomorrow, if I put metal to the pedal," replies Wheeljack.

Bulkhead is excited.

He has not seen Wheeljack in a long time.

But others also hear the message.

The Decepticons were listening the whole time!

They do not want Wheeljack to find the Autobots.

He is a hero who will help his friends.

Starscream has a plan to find out

the location of the Autobot base.

He calls for Makeshift, a giant, creepy robot.
Makeshift can do what no other robot can—
he can change forms
to look and sound like another robot!
The Decepticon begins to change.

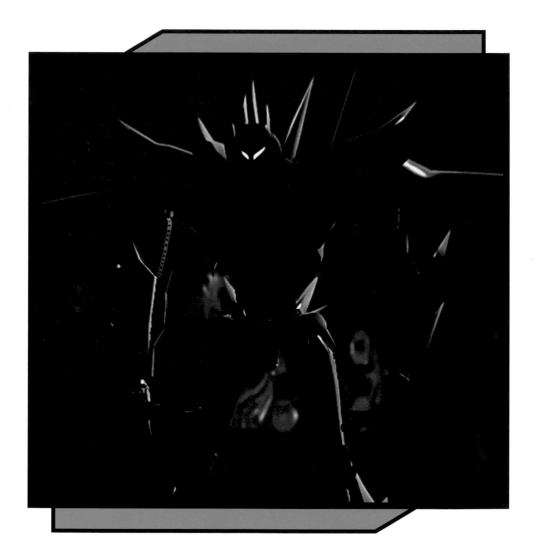

"I know how to prepare a warm welcome, too,"
says Starscream with an evil laugh.
"The Autobots will never suspect a thing."

At the base, everyone is talking

about Wheeljack's arrival.

The Autobots' human friends—Jack, Miko, and Raf—

are curious about this new Autobot.

"So Wheeljack is going to land somewhere else,

and then you'll bring him here?" asks Jack.

"Yes, we cannot risk revealing our location,

in case Wheeljack is being followed," replies Optimus.

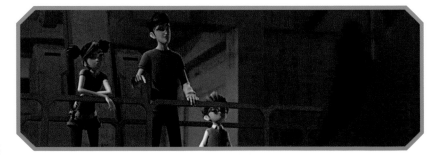

Arcee, Bulkhead, and Bumblebee use
the GroundBridge to meet Wheeljack.
The GroundBridge lets the Autobots travel
anywhere on Earth very quickly.
It also helps keep where their base is a secret.

Before the Autobots arrive at the meeting place,

the Decepticons attack Wheeljack!

"If you are going to try to ruin my day,"

says Wheeljack,

"you are going to have to try harder."

Wheeljack fights the Decepticons one by one.

He uses a pair of swords to battle.

By the time Bumblebee, Bulkhead, and Arcee reach Wheeljack, he has won the fight.

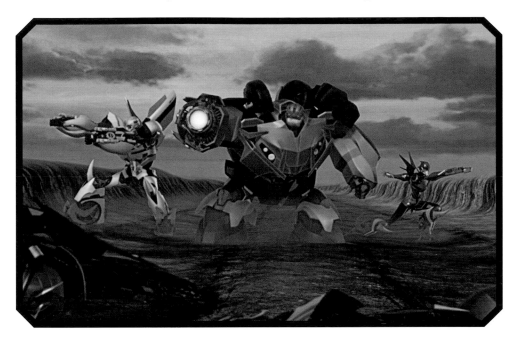

Bulkhead runs over and hugs his old friend. "Watch the finish, you old wrecking ball!" Wheeljack says with a laugh.

Back at the base, Wheeljack meets the other Autobots.

"It is an honor to meet you,"

says Wheeljack to Optimus Prime.

"Likewise, soldier," replies the Autobot leader.

He invites Wheeljack to stay with them.

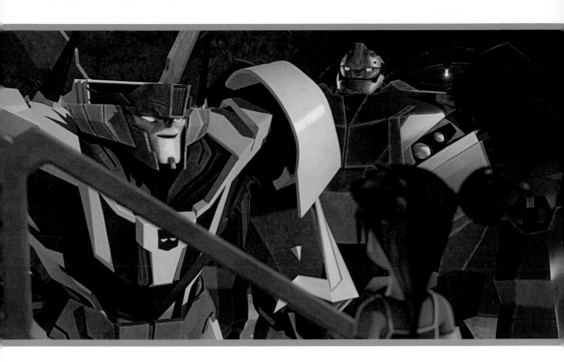

Wheeljack meets Miko,

Bulkhead's best human friend.

"Are you keeping Bulkhead out of trouble?"

Wheeljack asks.

"I try, but trouble finds us," Miko says.

Wheeljack laughs. Miko likes him.

Starscream is pleased that his plan is working.

He now has a spy inside the Autobot base.

The robot with the Autobots

is really Makeshift in disguise!

Starscream switched the Transformers during Wheeljack's fight with the Decepticons. The real Wheeljack is now tied up in the Decepticon base.

"Tell Megatron that he will not get away with this!" yells Wheeljack.

"Have you not heard? I lead the Decepticons now!" exclaims Starscream.

"You?" asks Wheeljack with a laugh.

"You will definitely not fool Bulkhead for long."

"Long enough to open the GroundBridge,"

replies Starscream.

"Then I can find the Autobots' base and destroy them!"

At the base, Makeshift is worried.

Ratchet has closed down the GroundBridge because it is broken.

He will need a few hours to make it work again.

Makeshift needs to find out where the base is
before his disguise no longer works!
"Besides the GroundBridge, is there any way
out of here?" Makeshift asks Miko.
"You are not planning to leave, are you?" Miko asks.
She is worried about Bulkhead.
"No," says Makeshift, lying.

Bulkhead notices that Wheeljack is acting strange.

Bulkhead asks the fake Wheeljack

to tell a story about one of their battles.

"Why do you want to live in the past?" asks Makeshift.

"Oh, come on, tell the story," prods Bulkhead.

The fake Wheeljack tells the story,

but he gets it wrong.

Now Bulkhead knows he is a fake!

Makeshift sees that he is in trouble.

He grabs Miko and tells the Autobots

that the Decepticons have the real Wheeljack.

He will not let go of Miko until the Decepticons arrive.

The GroundBridge is now up and running again.

Makeshift activates it for the Decepticons

to travel to the Autobot base.

Starscream's plan is working!

Soon the Decepticons will know where the base is

and will find the Autobots' human friends.

Except Starscream has not noticed
that the real Wheeljack has escaped!
Wheeljack sees the GroundBridge open
behind Starscream.

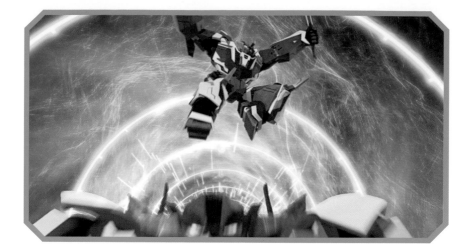

"Get him!" shouts Starscream to his troops.
But the real Wheeljack fights them with his swords
and escapes through the GroundBridge.
He finds his friends and comes face-to-face
with Makeshift, who still looks like him.
Everyone is shocked to see two Wheeljacks.
They look exactly the same!
Makeshift releases Miko
and prepares to battle Wheeljack.

"Time to take out the trash!" shouts the real Wheeljack. Bulkhead picks up Makeshift and throws him back through the GroundBridge.

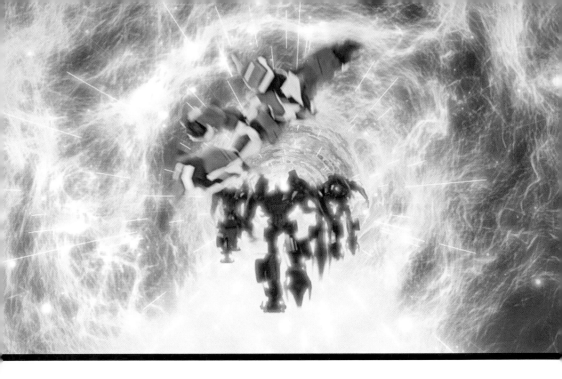

Makeshift flies through the portal.

He lands on top of a pile of Decepticon soldiers.

The gateway to the Autobot base closes

before they can cross over.

"Did you find out where the base is hidden?"

Starscream asks his spy.

Makeshift shakes his head.

Starscream is mad—they were so close!

The Autobots are happy their friend Wheeljack is safe.

Bulkhead wants him to stay with them,

but Wheeljack wants to go on more adventures.

He says good-bye to the Autobots for now.

He promises to come visit again soon!